Berry Fairy Tales

Rapunzel

Grosset & Dunlap

GROSSET & DUNLAP
Published by the Penguin Group
Penguin Group (USA) Inc., 375 Hudson Street, New York, New York 10014, U.S.A.
Penguin Group (Canada), 90 Eglinton Avenue East, Toronto, Ontario, Canada M4P 2Y3
(a division of Pearson Penguin Canada Inc.)
Penguin Books Ltd, 80 Strand, London WC2R 0RL, England
Penguin Ireland, 25 St Stephen's Green, Dublin 2, Ireland
(a division of Penguin Books Ltd)
Penguin Group (Australia), 250 Camberwell Road, Camberwell, Victoria 3124, Australia
(a division of Pearson Australia Group Pty Ltd)
Penguin Books India Pvt Ltd, 11 Community Centre, Panchsheel Park, New Delhi - 110 017, India
Penguin Group (NZ), 67 Apollo Drive, Mairangi Bay, Auckland 1311, New Zealand
(a division of Pearson New Zealand Ltd)
Penguin Books (South Africa) (Pty) Ltd, 24 Sturdee Avenue, Rosebank, Johannesburg 2196, South Africa

Penguin Books Ltd, Registered Offices:
80 Strand, London WC2R 0RL, England

Library of Congress Cataloging-in-Publication Data

Bryant, Megan E.
Rapunzel / by Megan E. Bryant ; illustrated by Tonja and John Huxtable.
p. cm. — (Berry fairy tales)
"Strawberry Shortcake."
Summary: An adaptation of the traditional tale, featuring Strawberry Shortcake and her friends.
ISBN 978-0-448-44556-4 (hardcover)
1. Fairy tales. 2. Folklore—Germany. I. Huxtable, Tonja, ill. II. Huxtable, John, ill. III. Rapunzel. English. IV. Title.
PZ8.B8425Rap 2007
398.2—dc22
E
2006031175

Special Markets ISBN 978-0-448-44780-3
Not for resale

Berry Fairy Tales

Rapunzel

By Megan E. Bryant
Illustrated by Tonja and John Huxtable

Grosset & Dunlap

Once upon a time, Strawberry Shortcake and her friends had a cookout in the Cinnamon Woods.

"Who's ready for dessert?" Blueberry Muffin asked after dinner. "I brought everything we need for s'mores!"

"All right!" cheered Huckleberry Pie. "I love s'mores!"

As the summer sun dipped beneath the trees, Orange Blossom shivered. "When—when do you think we'll go home?" she asked.

"We can't go home yet!" exclaimed Ginger Snap. "We haven't sung campfire songs or told scary stories—"

"Scary stories?" asked Orange. "Isn't it spooky enough in the woods?"

"I know a story that might make you feel better, Orange," Strawberry spoke up. "It's a little scary, so I'll only tell it if you are feeling berry brave."

"Okay," Orange said. "If you promise to hold my hand!"

Strawberry smiled as she reached out her hand. "Not so berry long ago . . ."

. . . a fair young maiden named Rapunzel lived in a cottage on the grounds of Berrymore Manor. Rapunzel had a gift for gardening, and was responsible for the care and keeping of the largest strawberry patch in Berry Kingdom.

"No one grows berries like you!" exclaimed Rapunzel's friend, Lady Ginger.

"I don't know how you do it," added Lord Huckleberry, master of the manor.

"Berries are like people," Rapunzel replied. "They need love to thrive."

But right next door to Berrymore Manor was a ramshackle old house where very little love bloomed. It was rumored that a wicked witch lived there, brewing all manner of sinister potions and terrible plans behind the cold stone walls.

Whenever Rapunzel passed by, she shivered and walked a little faster. No one wanted to cross paths with the wicked witch of Berry Kingdom.

One day, Rapunzel noticed that the rusted door in the wall around the witch's house had been left open. A soft green glow radiated from within. Overwhelmed by curiosity, Rapunzel peeked inside.

She found a garden filled with beautiful plants. "Oh, wonderful!" cried Rapunzel, forgetting about the witch as she spotted a plant under a glittering crystal cover. Berries red as jewels hung from its vines. Rapunzel held her breath as she reached out to touch the plant.

"How *dare* you?" shrieked a shrill voice. "How *dare* you?"

Startled, Rapunzel jumped away from the plant—and found herself
facing the witch! "I'm—I'm sorry," she stammered. "I didn't mean—"

"Get out!" the witch roared. "Never darken my doorway again!"

Blinded by tears, Rapunzel barely made it out of the witch's garden
before the iron door crashed shut behind her.

Rapunzel ran all the way home, her heart pounding and tears streaming down her face. By the time she was safely back at the manor, she was crying so hard that she could not speak.

"What is it, Rapunzel? What's wrong?" Lady Ginger asked, her voice full of worry.

"Slow down and tell us all about it," added Lord Huckleberry.

"I–I noticed that the gate next door was open," Rapunzel explained. "I peeked inside and found a pretty berry plant. But then the *witch* jumped out at me! And she told me to never darken her doorway again!"

"Oh, how dreadful!" said Lady Ginger. "You must never go back there."

Lord Huckleberry turned away, his face twisted in anger. "No one treats my friends like that," he vowed under his breath. "No one!"

That night, Lord Huckleberry snuck out of the manor. Silently, he stole into the witch's garden and found the plant that Rapunzel had described.

"If Rapunzel wants a berry from this plant, she'll get one," he muttered as he snatched a berry from the plant!

"Ha!" Lord Huckleberry exclaimed. "That will teach the witch a lesson about being nasty to nice people!"

Before Lord Huckleberry could take a single step, the plant crumbled into dust!

Lord Huckleberry stared at the pile of ashes in horror. *I've got to get away before the witch finds me here!* he thought. He raced back to the manor and dove into bed, trembling under the covers until morning.

At sunrise, the witch went to tend her most treasured plant—the crystal-covered berry bush. But when she reached it, a horrible sight met her eyes.

"Oh, *noooo*," moaned the witch. "My precious berries! Who did this, dear plant? What fool did not know that you are only to be touched during the first light of dawn?"

The witch's grief soon hardened to anger. "I know who brought this ruin upon my garden," she muttered. "That smug and spoiled Rapunzel from next door! She must—she *will*—pay for her crime!"

A nasty smile crossed the witch's face as she plotted her revenge. Without another word, she retreated to the tallest turret of her house—where she had a clear view of Rapunzel's cottage and berry patch.

After a breakfast of porridge, berries, and fresh cream, Rapunzel set off to tend her own berry patch. But as soon as she stepped among the berries, a bolt of purple lightning struck the ground at her feet. She fell to her knees. Billowing clouds of smoke swirled around her.

"What—what's happening?" Rapunzel cried. "Help! Help!"

When the smoke cleared, Rapunzel found herself trapped in a tall tower!
"I warned you not to touch my plant," sneered the witch.
"You must be mistaken!" protested Rapunzel. "I didn't touch anything!"
But without another word, the witch vanished in a cloud of smoke.
Rapunzel tried to find a way out of the tower. But there were no doors, and
the drop from the only window was too dangerous. "Will I never escape from this
prison?" Rapunzel sobbed before crying herself to sleep.

As the days turned into weeks, Rapunzel stopped searching for a way out of the tower. The witch visited Rapunzel every day, bringing food and small trinkets to make her happy. One afternoon, she surprised Rapunzel with a bowl of sweet strawberries. "I love berries!" Rapunzel exclaimed.

"So do I," the witch said shyly.

As they shared the berries, Rapunzel couldn't help but think that the witch might have been her friend—if only things were different.

As Lord Huckleberry and Lady Ginger searched the Berry Kingdom for their missing friend, they spotted a tall tower. When they hid in the brush, they saw a cloaked figure approach the tower. "Rapunzel! Rapunzel! Let down your hair!" a voice called.

A long, red braid tumbled out the tower window. As the figure climbed up the braid, its hood fell back to reveal the witch!

"Rapunzel!" whispered Lady Ginger. "We must rescue her!"

"We will," replied Lord Huckleberry.

Rapunzel's friends spent the long night weaving a strong and sturdy rope of vines. At last, it was time for the rescue to begin.

"After the moon sets, we have an hour until dawn," Lord Huckleberry whispered. "It should be just enough time to rescue Rapunzel!"

Lady Ginger nodded. She threw the rope as high as she could and watched it twist into a tight knot around the top of the tower. Silently, Lady Ginger and Lord Huckleberry climbed up to Rapunzel's room.

"Rapunzel! Rapunzel!" Lady Ginger cried. "Wake up!"

Rapunzel sleepily rubbed her eyes. "Oh, my friends!" she gasped. "It's so good to see you again!"

"We've come to rescue you," Lord Huckleberry said. "Let's get out of here!"

But Rapunzel shook her head. "No."

Lord Huckleberry stared at her in amazement. "What are you talking about? We've got to leave—*now!*"

Suddenly the tower filled with smoke. "You're not going anywhere!" the witch's voice rang out as she appeared before them. "After all the kindness I've shown you, *this* is how you repay me? By running away?"

"No!" cried Rapunzel. "I wasn't—"

"Stop lying to me!" the witch yelled. "I should have known better than to trust you. First you destroy my berry plant—"

"Rapunzel didn't destroy your plant," Lord Huckleberry interrupted. "I did. I only wanted to take a berry for Rapunzel to make her feel better, but that was wrong. And I should have confessed when it happened. I—I apologize."

"And Rapunzel wasn't going to run away," added Lady Ginger. "We came here to rescue her—but she wouldn't leave."

The witch turned to Rapunzel. "Is this true?" she asked.

Rapunzel nodded. "I wouldn't leave without saying good-bye," she said.

"I never should have locked you in the tower," the witch said. "Or yelled at you when I found you in my garden. I've made some terrible mistakes."

"We all have," Rapunzel said. "If we had taken the time to get to know you, maybe this trouble could have been avoided. Can you forgive us?"

"Yes—but only if you can forgive me. I promise I won't use any more enchantments—ever. And you should know that my real name is Orangetta," their new friend said shyly.

The friends walked home together as the sun started to rise.

"Would you come into my garden?" Orangetta asked. She led her friends to a crystal case.

"This is my new berry plant," Orangetta explained. "And since the first light of dawn is here, we can each have a berry without harming the plant!"

Rapunzel smiled at Orangetta. She just knew that they would soon be the berry best of friends . . .

". . . and live berry happily ever after!" Strawberry announced as she finished her story.

"So the witch wasn't a real witch?" Orange Blossom asked.

"Not at all," replied Strawberry.

"I think I understand why you told that story, Strawberry," Orange said. "Scary things aren't always as scary as they seem—right?"

"That's right!" Strawberry exclaimed.

"Just like that spooky shape over there is a shadow—not a monster," Orange continued. "And that howling noise is just the wind—not a pack of ghosts."

Blueberry Muffin shivered. "Now you're starting to scare me, Orange!"

"Me, too!" added Ginger. "Why don't you tell a scary story now?"

Orange Blossom's eyes twinkled. "It was a dark and stormy night," she began.

Strawberry smiled. She wasn't afraid—as long as her best friends were nearby!